This book is dedicated to Matthew,
our own little Farfalla.

Acknowledgements

Kristin Blackwood
Mike Blanc
Kurt Landefeld
Paul Royer
Jennie Levy Smith
Sheila Tarr
Michael Olin-Hitt
Carolyn Brodie
Elaine Mesek

FARFALLA
VanitaBooks, LLC

Text by Vanita Oelschlager
Illustrations by Kristin Blackwood
Design by Mike Blanc

Hardcover Edition ISBN 978-0-9832904-0-7 Paperback Edition ISBN 978-0-9832904-3-8

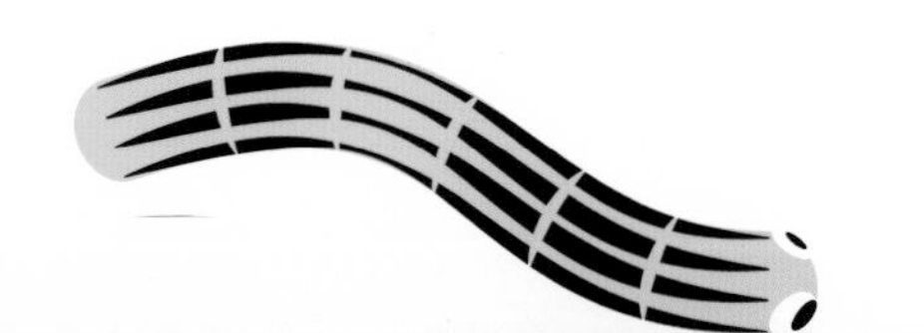

www.VanitaBooks.com

Farfalla

A Story of Loss and Hope

with Story by

Vanita Oelschlager

and Art by

Kristin Blackwood

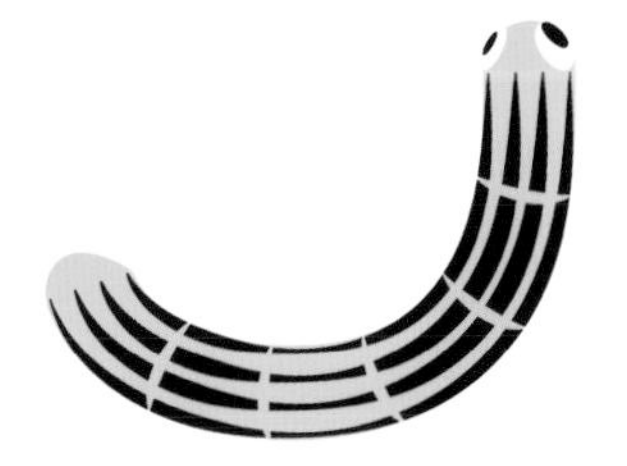

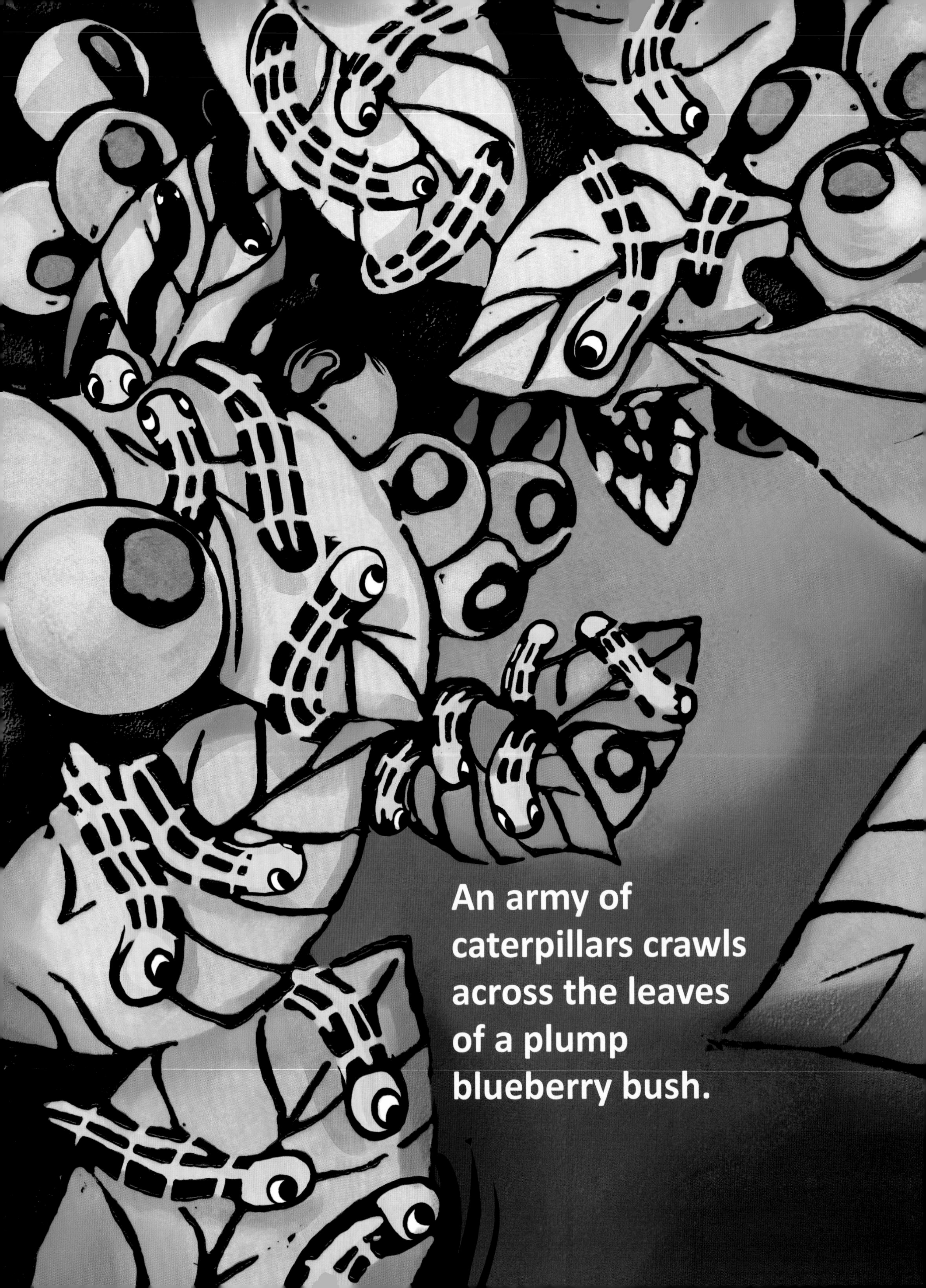

An army of
caterpillars crawls
across the leaves
of a plump
blueberry bush.

A little beetle and his mother come into the garden and notice the caterpillars.

Little Beetle crawls closer to the group of caterpillars for a better look.

The mother busies herself in a puddle of mud.

The group of fuzzy caterpillars and the
little beetle regard each other with curiosity.

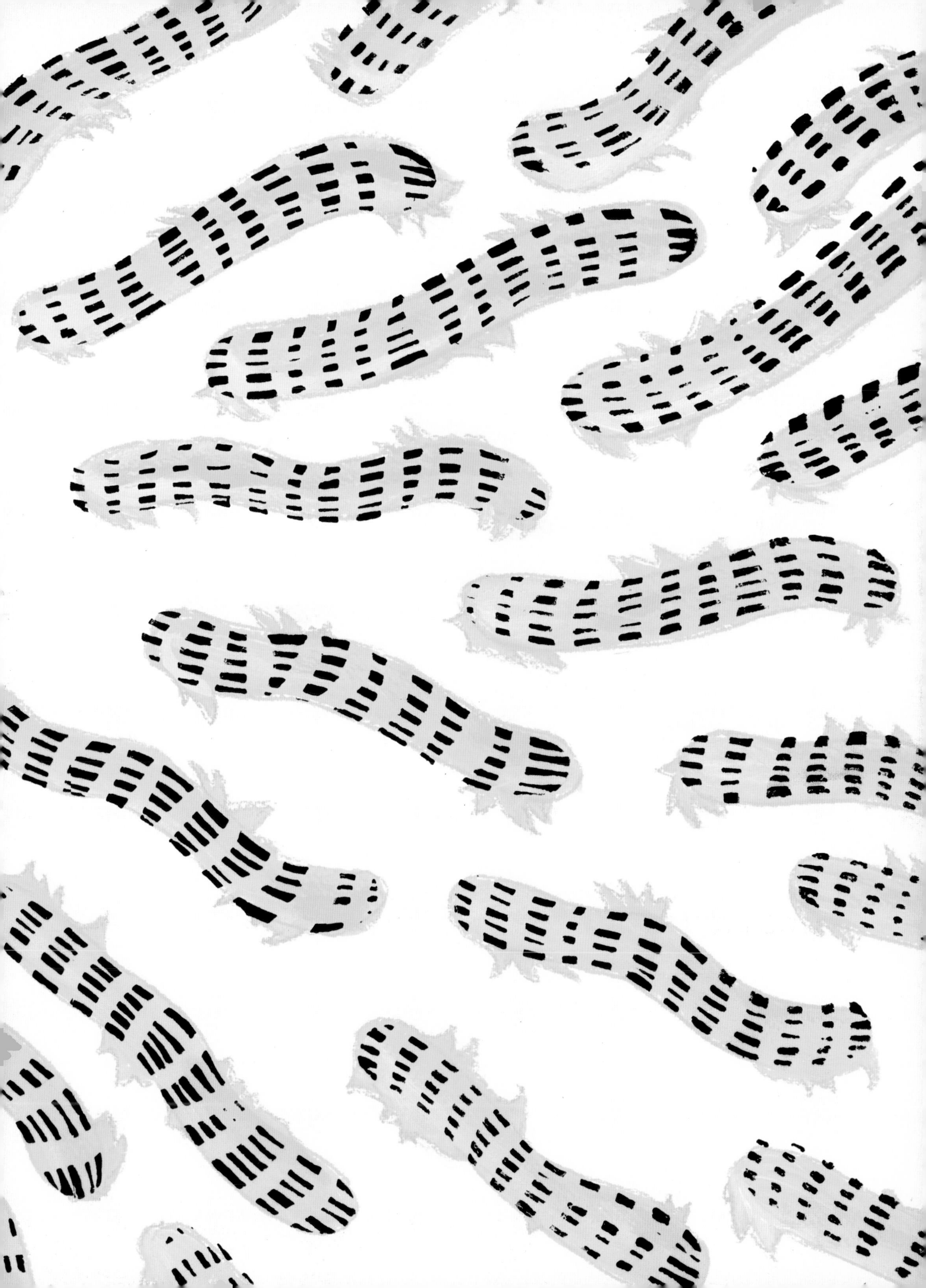

The squirming caterpillars crawl up on to the little beetle.

Their fur is soft.
The little beetle giggles at their touch.

"Tee Hee Hee"

The days of summer are bright and warm. Little Beetle comes to the garden to play with his new friends.

One day, Little Beetle and his mother arrive, only to find the garden empty.

He searches on the blueberry leaves,
but his friends are gone.

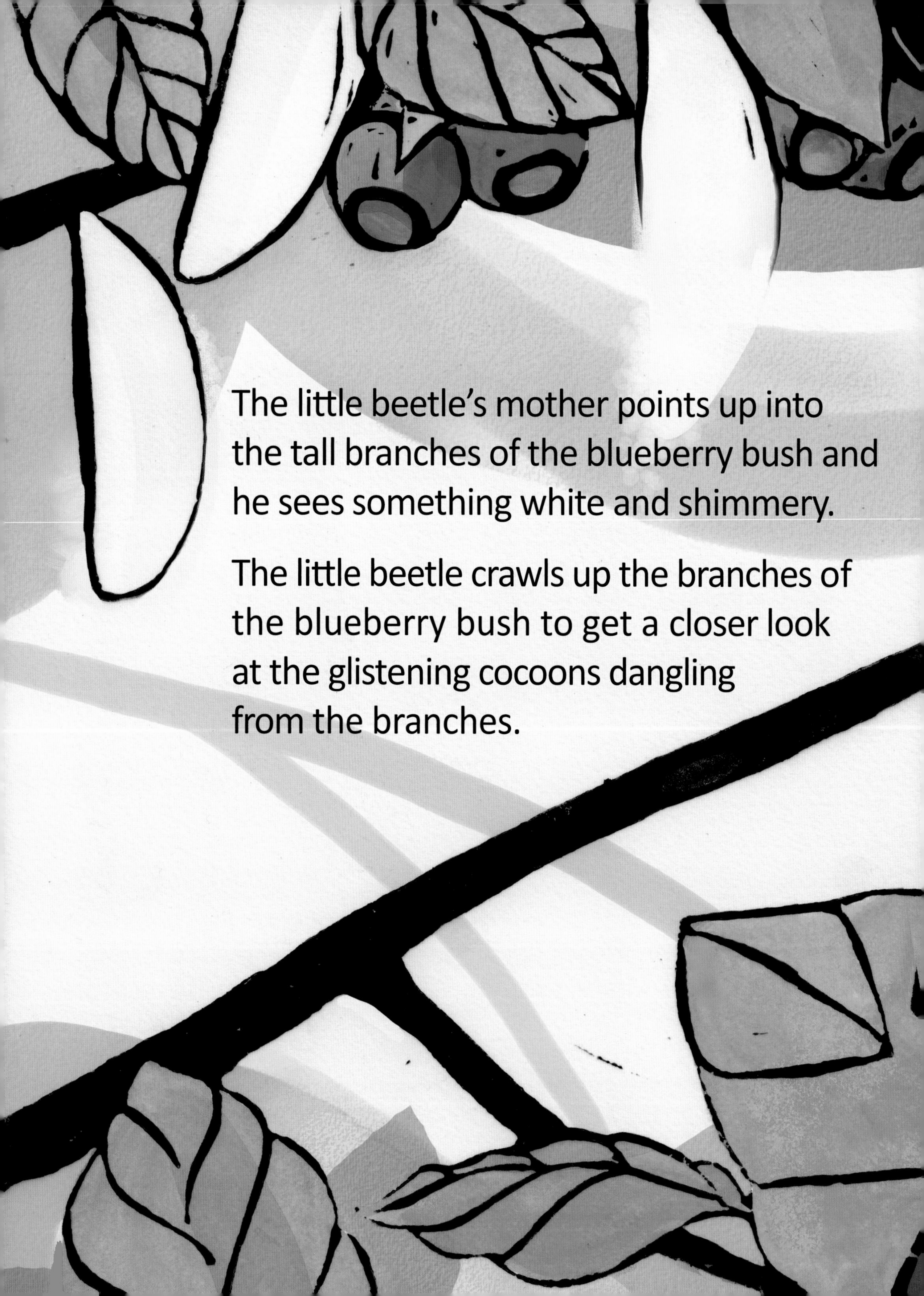

The little beetle's mother points up into the tall branches of the blueberry bush and he sees something white and shimmery.

The little beetle crawls up the branches of the blueberry bush to get a closer look at the glistening cocoons dangling from the branches.

"If you are patient, says Mother Beetle,
"You will be rewarded with a special surprise...

butterflies."

Little Beetle begins to think of all the fun he will have with the butterflies when they come out of their cocoons.

They will ride on his back.

They will join together and lift him into the sky.

Little Beetle is very patient and waits.

And waits.

And waits . . .

until one sunny morning . . .

. . . the shimmering cocoons begin to vibrate with excitement!

Little Beetle sees the first of the brightly colored wings poke through the cocoon.

The butterflies dance around the garden and fly up and away until they have all flown off.

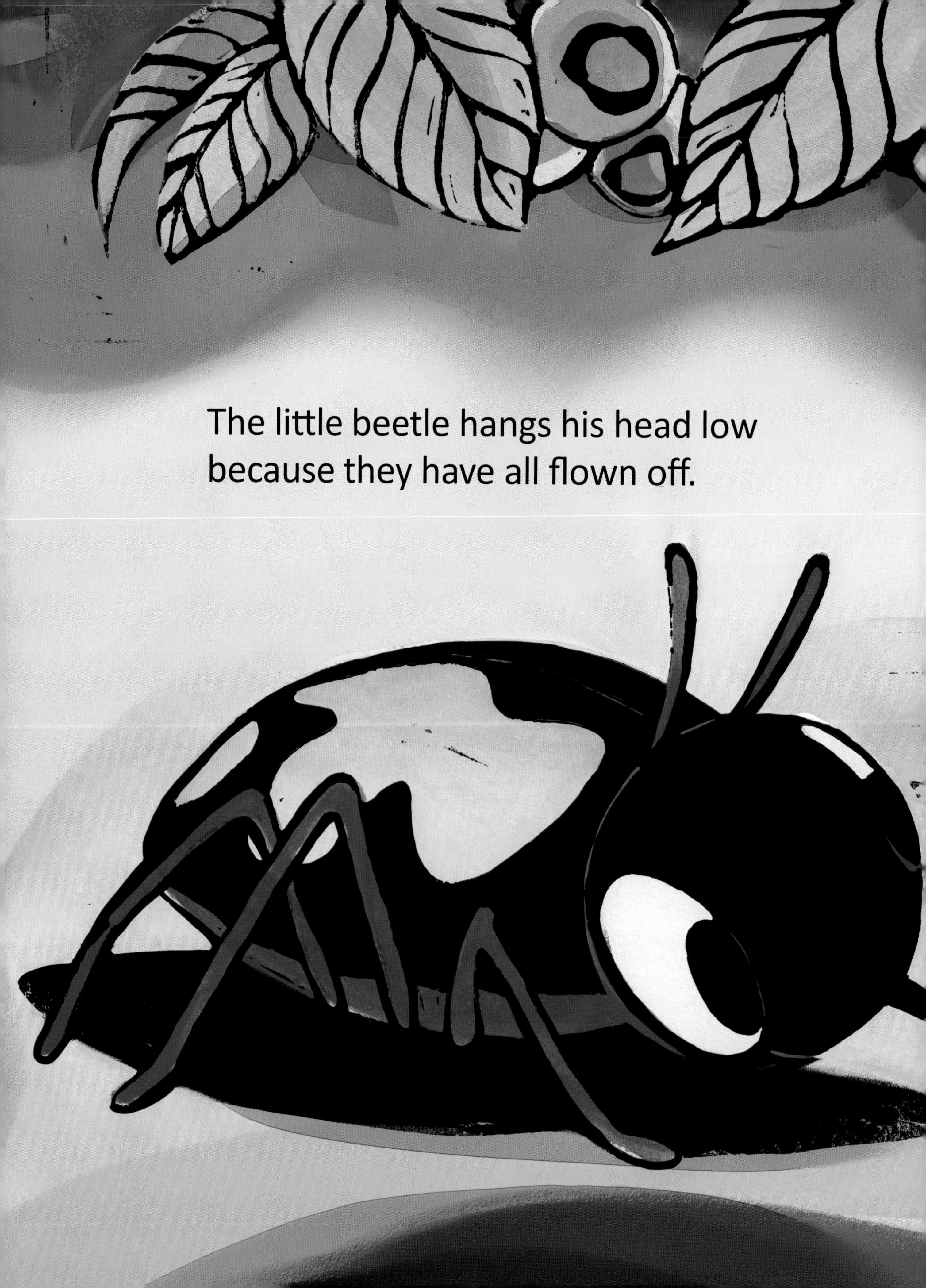

The little beetle hangs his head low
because they have all flown off.

Mother Beetle says, “Look up, Little Beetle.
There is one more cocoon left.”

Little Beetle sits and waits for his butterfly

He talks to the cocoon.

He makes plans.

Little Beetle names the butterfly-to-be Farfalla.

Day after day the little beetle waits . . .

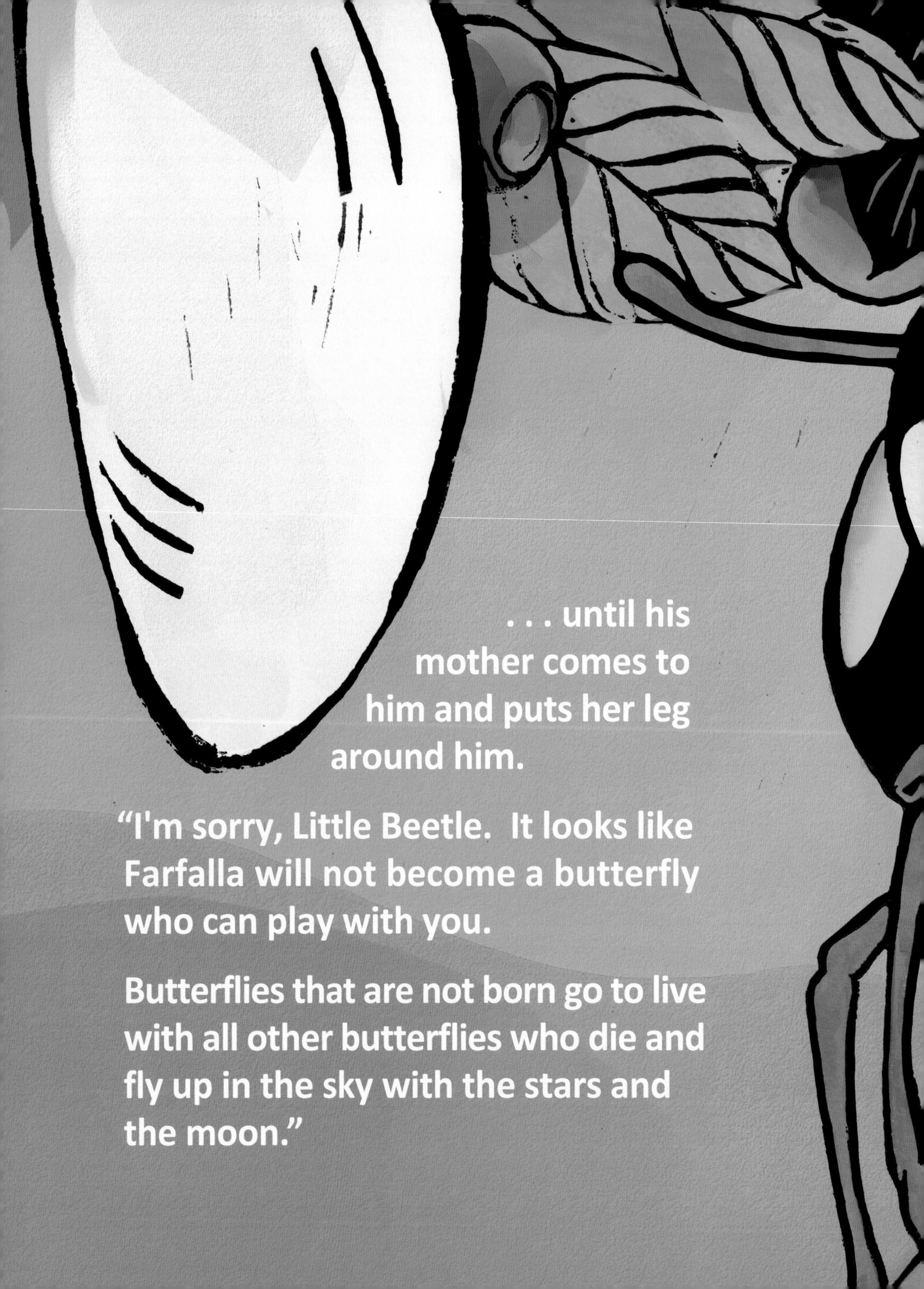

. . . until his
mother comes to
him and puts her leg
around him.

"I'm sorry, Little Beetle. It looks like Farfalla will not become a butterfly who can play with you.

Butterflies that are not born go to live with all other butterflies who die and fly up in the sky with the stars and the moon."

Little Beetle does not want to believe this is true.

He has waited so long for this special butterfly to emerge from its cocoon.

“Will I go to the moon and the stars when I die? Will I see Farfalla then?” Little Beetle asks his mother.

“We will all go to the stars and the moon when we die.” says Mother Beetle with a hug.

"Goodbye Farfalla."
Little Beetle says
with a sniffle.

Farfalla flutters his wings and watches Little Beetle from high in the sky.

Little Beetle looks up to Farfalla from the blueberry bush down in the garden.

Author

Vanita Oelschlager is a wife, mother, grandmother, philanthropist, former teacher, current caregiver, author and poet. A graduate of the University of Mount Union in Alliance, Ohio, she now serves as a Trustee of her alma mater and as Writer in Residence for the Literacy Program at The University of Akron. Vanita and her husband Jim were honored with a *Lifetime Achievement Award* from the National Multiple Sclerosis Society in 2006. She was the Congressional *Angels in Adoption™ Award* recipient for the State of Ohio in 2007 and was named *National Volunteer of the Year* by the MS Society in 2008. Vanita was also honored in 2009 as the *Woman Philanthropist of the Year* by the United Way of Summit County. In May 2011, Vanita received an honorary Doctor of Humane Letters from the University of Mount Union.

Net Profits

All net profits from this book will be donated to charitable organizations, with a gentle preference toward those serving people with my husband's disease – Multiple Sclerosis.

Vanita

Artist

Kristin Blackwood is a teacher and frequent illustrator of books for children. Her works of art are published in: *My Grampy Can't Walk*, *Let Me Bee*, *What Pet Will I Get?*, *Made in China*, *Big Blue*, *Ivy in Bloom*, *Ivan's Great Fall*, *A Tale of Two Daddies* and *Bonyo Bonyo*. A graduate of Kent State University, Kristin has a degree in Art History. When she isn't designing or teaching, she enjoys being a mother to her two daughters.